D1284589

Duke
THE BEAR DETECTIVE™

Case #2
Poker and the Cupcake Chase
By Raymond Coutu
Illustrated by Renée Graef

Published by Bear & Company Publications
Copyright © 2002 by Bear & Company

Printed in the United States of America

Duke The Bear Detective™ is a registered trademark of
Bear & Company.

Based on a series concept by Dawn Jones
Edited by Dawn Jones
Designed by Valerie Hodgson

Library of Congress Cataloging-in-Publication Data

Coutu, Raymond.
Poker and the cupcake chase / written by Raymond Coutu ;
illustrations by Renée Graef.
p. cm. -- (Duke, the bear detective ; case #2)
"Based on a series concept by Dawn L. Jones."
Summary: When forest friends gather to celebrate the opening of
Duke the bear's detective agency, they discover that Poker the
porcupine is missing and so are the cupcakes
he promised to bring.
ISBN 0-9712840-7-5 (pbk. : alk. paper)
[1. Bears--Fiction. 2. Porcupines--Fiction. 3. Forest animals--
Fiction.
4. Missing persons--Fiction. 5. Mystery and detective stories.]
I. Graef, Renée, ill. II. Jones, Dawn L., 1963- III. Title.
PZ7.C83315 Po 2001
[Fic]--dc21
2001005152

For John
Raymond Coutu

For Max
Renée Graef

Message to Parents

Bear & Company, part of
The Boyds Collection, Ltd. family, is
committed to creating quality reading and play
experiences that inspire kids to learn, imagine,
and explore the world around them.
Working together with experienced children's
authors, illustrators, and educators, we
promise to create stories and products that are
respectful to your children and that will earn
your respect in turn.

Chapter One

Duke was a curious bear. He was also a bear with too much time on his hands. So when his friend Poker told him to become a detective, Duke thought it was a brilliant idea–so brilliant, in fact, that he opened his own detective agency and threw a big party to celebrate.

The party was the event of the season. Everyone came with yummy things to eat. Babette the rabbit brought a pie made from apples she had grown herself. Felix the fox brought hamburgers.

Jessie, *The Daily Log's* cub reporter and one of Duke's best friends, brought her famous peanut butter cookies. And there were other guests, too–Rodney the raccoon, Barbara the sheep, Vernon the beaver, and all of Vernon's lodge brothers.

When the party was underway, Duke stood on a wooden crate to give a toast. He raised his cup of cider and said, "I'd like to thank you all for coming. Especially Poker, who gave me the idea to open my own detective agency in the first place." Duke scanned the guests for his porcupine friend, but couldn't spot him.

"Poker?" he called out. No one answered. "Poker, are you out there?"

"Maybe he's in the kitchen," said Barbara.

"Maybe he's in the bathroom," said Vernon.

"No, I didn't see him arrive," Jessie replied. "And I was in charge of greeting guests."

"And Poker was in charge of bringing cupcakes!" cried Felix, slipping off of his scooter.

With that, the crowd became very worried. After all, what's a party without cupcakes?

"I'll get to the bottom of this," said Duke, stepping down from the crate. The crowd parted as he made his way inside to the telephone. He dialed Poker. One ring, two rings, three rings—no answer. "Where could he be?" Duke wondered as he pulled his hat, coat, and magnifying glass from the wardrobe and rejoined the group outside.

"Well?" Felix asked.

Duke stared at the guests seriously.
"Poker's either on his way here, or..."
The guests stared back at him nervously.

"Or what?" Jessie asked.

"Or he's missing," said Duke.

The guests gasped.

"Come with me, Jessie. I need your help."

"Where are we going?"

"To solve our first official mystery."

Chapter Two

The two bears reached the grassy path that led to the tree where Poker lived. They started down it, running as fast as they could.

When they were about halfway to Poker's tree, Jessie had to stop to catch her breath.

Duke stopped, too–and like any good detective, examined the scene more closely. "Jessie, something's not right about this path," he said.

"What do you mean?" she asked, taking a deep breath.

"Look at the grass ahead of us."

She did. "So?"

With magnifying glass in hand, Duke fell to his knees for a closer look. "These blades are standing straight up and down."

Jessie was getting impatient. "That's how grass usually grows, Duke!"

"Poker wasn't on this path today. If he had been, what would the grass look like?"

Jessie thought it over for a moment, "Trampled?"

"Exactly," Duke replied, "especially with Poker's waist size."

Jessie nodded. "Good point. So he never even tried to get to the party?"

"At least not on this path."

Jessie removed her reporter's notebook from her backpack, jotted down the clue, and continued on with Duke.

When they arrived at Poker's tree, Duke approached its big, red door. One knock, two knocks, three knocks–no answer.

The two bears looked at each other.

"What now?" Jessie asked.

Duke crouched down. "Poker, are you in there?" he called through the keyhole. But no one answered.

"Try the knob," Jessie urged.

Duke knew that it was rude to enter somebody's home without being asked, but this was a special case: Poker was missing. When Duke tried to open the door, though, he couldn't. It was locked.

"What now?" Jessie asked again.

Duke scanned the tree and spotted the window above the door. "Get on my shoulders," he told Jessie.

"Why?"

Duke flicked his bear chin upward. "For a look inside."

Jessie smiled and climbed up. Once she caught her balance, she peered through the glass.

"What do you see?" Duke asked, trying to stay steady.

"A big mess. He should hire a housekeeper."

Now Duke was getting impatient. "Jessie, do you see anything suspicious?"

17

She started looking with a reporter's eye. "Wait a minute…," she whispered.

"What?" Duke asked.

"There are baking supplies on the table–muffin tins, mixing bowls, measuring spoons."

"Sounds like everything you need to make cupcakes."

Jessie climbed down from Duke's shoulders. "Yes, except for one thing."

"What?"

"Think about it," she said, writing in her notebook.

"Ingredients?"

"Right," Jessie answered.

Clue #2
Baking supplies,
but no ingredients.
So how could
Poker make
cupcakes?

19

Chapter Three

"But how could Poker make cupcakes without ingredients?" Duke asked.

"He couldn't," Jessie said. "He'd have to buy what he needs."

Duke thought about it, and then his eyes popped wide. "The market!"

"That's my guess," Jessie said.

Off the two bears went again, this time through the forest to the North Village, where all the shops were located. Jessie knew a shortcut that Poker had shown her.

Along the way, at a turn in the
path, something caught Duke's
attention. It looked a bit like an
extra-long pine needle. He picked
it up.

"What's that, Duke?" Jessie asked.

Duke looked at the object through
his magnifying glass. "Maybe an
old pine needle."

Jessie took a closer look. "It's a strange-looking pine needle. There's a little barb at the tip. What else could it be?"

"A porcupine quill?" Duke wondered.

"Do you think so? One of Poker's?" Jessie asked.

"Maybe."

Jessie sketched the object in her notebook and wrote herself another note.

When the two bears got to the market, they went directly to the baking goods aisle to look for Poker. But there was no sign of him. The only one there was Beau, the stock bear, pricing bags of flour. So Duke asked him, "Have you seen a porcupine here today?"

"What does he look like?" asked Beau.

Duke searched for gentle words to describe his friend: "He's kind of short and brown and round–"

"He could use a bath," Jessie cut in.

Beau tapped his cheek and thought about it. "Oh, you mean Poker!"

"Yes, Poker," Duke said. "Have you seen him?"

"He was here earlier, shopping for cupcake ingredients..."

Duke and Jessie smiled proudly
at each other.

"…but he didn't buy anything."

Their smiles wilted. "Why?"
Duke asked.

"Too much work," Beau said. "I told him how many ingredients he'd need, and how long it would take to make the cupcakes. Then he said, 'Forget it.'"

"Did he say anything else?" asked Jessie, like a true reporter.

Beau started tapping his cheek again. "Not really. Just that it would be easier to buy the cupcakes already made."

Duke looked at Jessie from the corner of his eye. "Are you thinking what I'm thinking?"

Jessie nodded. "The bakery."

Chapter Four

The bears made a beeline for the bakery. But when they arrived at its doorstep, they found a sign they didn't expect:

Sorry, We're Closed.

The baker had shut down shop only ten minutes earlier.

Jessie hung her bear head. "We'll never see Poker again."

Duke put his arm around her shoulder. "What have I told you about 'never'?"

Jessie looked at him. "Never say it?"

"Right," said Duke. "We'll find Poker."

"But we're at a dead end, Duke."

Duke looked around. He was searching for something, anything, that could point them toward their friend. Nothing caught his eye–but something sure caught his nose. Something sweet, coming from behind the building.

As Duke and Jessie followed the scent, they noticed trash scattered on the ground. "Boy, that baker should learn to clean up before he shuts down. What a mess!" Duke said.

"It *is* a mess," Jessie said with a smile. "A glorious mess."

Duke looked at her, confused. "What are you talking about?"

"Who makes the best mess around?"

"Poker!" Duke cried. He pulled out his magnifying glass for a closer look at the trash.

"What do you see?" Jessie asked.

"Crumpled cupcake cups," said Duke.

Jessie took out her notebook and recorded the finding. "Used or unused?"

"Definitely used." Duke scanned the whole area. "And they form a trail. Whoever dropped them was going somewhere."

The two bears followed the trail of cupcake cups into the forest, hoping that Poker would be at its end. But all the trail led them to was an old, hollow log. Nothing more.

"Now what?" asked Jessie.

Duke didn't have a clue. So he sat down on the log to gather his thoughts. But something jabbed his bottom.

"Ouch!" Duke cried, jumping up like a jack-in-the-box. "What was that?"

After rubbing the sting away, Duke inspected the log where

he'd sat down. He saw a spear-shaped object sticking out from a hole.

"Was it a bee?" Jessie asked.

"Nope," Duke said. "Please hand me the sketch you did earlier."

Jessie opened her notebook to the right page and gave it to Duke.

Duke looked at the sketch and then looked inside the hollow log to find a familiar face waking from a nap. "Just as I suspected!" Duke said. "It was a porcupine quill!"

Poker poked his head from the end of the log.

"We've been looking all over for you!" Jessie squealed.

"Is it almost time for the party?" Poker yawned.

"The party started over an hour ago–without you," Duke answered. "What are you doing here? We were counting on you for the cupcakes."

The porcupine crawled out of

the log and stretched. "Well," he explained. "I was going to bake some, but then I realized I didn't have the ingredients."

"Or the desire," said Duke, arms crossed.

"That, too," Poker agreed. "So I bought some cupcakes at the bakery. But on my way to the party, I decided to try them before serving them to guests. That's the proper thing to do, after all."

"How many did you *try*?" Duke asked, arms still crossed.

Poker looked at him, embarrassed. "All of them."

"And you made a mess," Jessie scolded. "You shouldn't litter."

"Or eat so many cupcakes so quickly," Poker said. "I felt pretty sick. So I decided to curl up for a little sleep–to settle my tummy. Guess I overslept."

"Guess you did," Duke growled.

"I'm sorry," said Poker. "Can I still come to your party?"

Jessie nudged Duke.

He dropped his arms and cast his eyes skyward. "Oh, all right!"

Poker flashed a sleepy, thankful grin.

"It wouldn't be a party without you," Duke said, giving his good friend his best bear hug.

The three animals headed back to Duke's.

Chapter Five

Duke and Jessie arrived to find the guests still gathered.

"Where are the cupcakes?" Felix asked.

"There will be no cupcakes, I'm afraid," Duke said. "But I brought something even better."

With that, Poker stepped out from behind a blueberry bush, looking quite guilty. The guests

greeted him with great relief.

"We thought we'd never see you again," said Barbara.

"Thank goodness you're safe," said Vernon.

"Yes, thank goodness," Felix agreed. "But *why* will there be no cupcakes?!"

"It's a long story," said Duke.

"I'm more of a meatloaf man, anyway," said the young fox, scanning the food table. "And there isn't much here for me." With that, he hopped aboard his scooter and zipped off.

Duke took his place on the crate to finish his toast. "Now that we're all here, I want to thank you for coming." He then cleared his throat and became very serious. "The forest holds many mysteries, too many for one bear to solve alone. So it's my honor to appoint two new agents. Jessie and Poker, please come forward."

Jessie and Poker did as they were told, with smiles as wide as melon slices.

"To my new partners," Duke said, placing official detective caps on their heads. "Welcome aboard!"

Jessie and Poker thanked him, and then turned to Barbara for a photo.

Cheers filled the air. It was a magic moment. If any of their

forest friends needed a mystery
solved, Duke and his agents
would be on the case. They were
a team.

The Facts
Behind
The Clues

*Why doesn't grass
"save" footprints?*

When grass is trampled, it can show
footprints. But they don't last long
because of the way grass grows.
Grass roots grow downward due to
the earth's pull. Grass blades grow
upward, toward the sun. After grass
is trampled, it soon straightens up to
move toward the sun once again.
This kind of plant movement is
called tropism.

A porcupine's barbed quills help protect it from predators such as fishers, coyotes, and great horned owls. When a porcupine senses danger, his quills stand on end and become loose. If he's attacked, he releases a load of quills, usually from his tail, into the attacker's flesh. The barbs prevent the quills from falling out easily. Ouch!

The Facts Behind The Clues

Why did Duke sniff the trail of cupcake cups before he saw it?

Few animals have a better sense of smell than the bear. In fact, some scientists believe that bears rely on their noses as much as we rely on our eyes. Like all mammals, bears have special cells in their snouts called sensory receptors. These cells are so good at "catching" smells that bears can communicate with one another through scent marking. They rub against trees to leave scents that let other bears know when they're ready to mate and to mark their territories.

Porcupines rely on trees as a place to live and as a source of food. They're known to make dens in hollow logs and feed on almost every part of every kind of tree–the bark, the buds, the leaves, and the wood inside. And, like Poker, porcupines are lazy. Rather than moving from tree to tree, they'd rather just sit in one and munch on it for days!

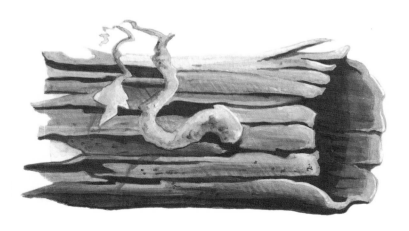